The Terrible Orchid Sky

Anne Schraff

PAGETURNERS

ADVENTURE

A Horse Called Courage

Planet Doom

The Terrible Orchid Sky

Up Rattler Mountain

Who Has Seen the Beast?

MYSTERY

The Hunter

Once Upon a Crime

Whatever Happened to Megan Marie?

When Sleeping Dogs Awaken

Where's Dudley?

Development and Production: Laurel Associates, Inc.
Cover Illustrator: Black Eagle Productions

Copyright © 2001 by Saddleback Publishing, Inc. All rights reserved. No part of this publication may be reproduced or transmitted in any form without permission in writing from the publisher. Reproduction of any part of this book, through photocopy, recording, or any electronic or mechanical retrieval system, without the written permission of the publisher, is an infringement of copyright law.

SADDLEBACK
PUBLISHING · INC.
Three Watson
Irvine, CA 92618-2767

E-Mail: info@sdlback.com
Website: www.sdlback.com

ISBN 1-56254-185-4

Printed in the United States of America
05 04 03   9 8 7 6 5 4 3 2 1

CONTENTS

Chapter 1 5

Chapter 2 11

Chapter 3 18

Chapter 4 25

Chapter 5 32

Chapter 6 38

Chapter 7 44

Chapter 8 51

Chapter 9 58

Chapter 10 66

Chapter 1

Ken Talbot was 18 when he started junior college.

"These days you won't get anywhere without college, boy," his stepdad had told him gruffly. Ken knew that the man didn't think much of his prospects anyway. Once Ken had heard him saying, "That kid's a real loser, just like his father."

But junior college turned out to be just like high school; Ken hated it. He didn't like being stuck in boring classes, listening to teachers yakking away. What he really wanted to do was get out of there as fast as he could.

When Ken quit college, his stepdad had said, "I knew you wouldn't stick it out. You're a lazy good-for-nothing kid." Ken couldn't take it anymore. He had never liked George Garvin much, and now he liked him even less.

"I'm outta here, Mom. I'm going to Florida," Ken said.

"Ken," Mom said, "don't be a fool. Your father never amounted to a hill of beans because he was a quitter. That's why I had to leave him. Now you're turning out just like him. If you go to Florida, you'll just learn *more* bad habits from him!"

Ken hitched up his backpack and kissed his mother goodbye. That afternoon he was on a bus headed for Florida. As long as he used earphones, he could listen to his favorite rap music without bothering the other passengers. Ken listened to hard-driving rap all the way from Michigan to Florida.

Ken was angry. He'd been angry for about as long as he could remember. For

Chapter · 1

some reason, though, rap music seemed to soothe him. Maybe it was because rap sounded even madder than he was.

Ken got to wondering what his father was like these days. Ken was about 12 the last time he saw him. Dad was a fisherman then, a beachcomber, or, as Mom liked to say, "a bum." He worked at whatever he could find, and sometimes he didn't work at all. He was the exact opposite of Ken's stepdad. George Garvin was a good plumber and a steady worker.

Ken got off the bus in a little south Florida town called Breeze End. Funny, Ken thought, is this where the breezes end? It didn't seem like it. A stiff wind was blowing right now. All the palm trees were bowing their graceful crowns.

Ken didn't see many people on the street. Where was everybody? Sure, he knew it was just a small town, but still there should have been *some* action. Ken passed a gas station, a grocery store, and two 99¢ stores. When he'd called his father to say he was coming, Dad had said his house was just beyond a tackle and bait shop. "You can't miss it," he had said. "It's a white frame house with purple trim—number 3 Breeze Way."

Sure enough, there it was! Ken grinned, feeling relaxed already. The house looked like Dad: unkempt, with junk lying around the front yard. No wonder a neatnik like Mom couldn't stand him for long. Mom had remarried when Ken was about five. The other two kids now in the family were George Garvin's children. They were big kids, good athletes, and they made great grades in school. They were all the things Ken was not.

Ken never felt like he belonged in the neat, clean Garvin household. He felt like something left over from nasty old Ed Talbot—some junk that Talbot had

Chapter • 1

forgotten to take with him when he was kicked out. Dad hadn't left much behind—just a few old tackle boxes, some windbreakers, and Ken. Sometimes Ken felt that when Mom threw out Dad's stuff, she would've liked to have thrown him out, too. *For sure* George Garvin would've liked to have seen Ken out of there.

Ken went up to the door. The whole little house seemed to rattle like an old skeleton when he knocked on the door. Suddenly, Ken felt a little nervous. He hadn't seen Dad since he was about 12. Every time Dad had come north to visit Ken, there had been a big fight between him and Ken's mom.

Ever since the divorce Mom had wanted nothing to do with Ed Talbot. She was afraid his presence would be a bad influence on Ken. So she had devoted her life to keeping father and son apart.

Then the front door swung open, interrupting Ken's uneasy memories. A grizzled face looked out and barked, "Yeah? What do you want?"

Chapter 2

Ken gasped. The man standing before him was so much older than Ken had remembered him! His once crow's wing black hair was gray now. Some of it was almost white. The man was a little thinner too, and his beard was gray, streaked with white.

But the biggest surprise was that Dad didn't recognize him at once. Ken had never thought about how much he must have changed since he was 12. "Hi, Dad, it's me," Ken said. "It's your kid."

The man drew back, looking the boy up and down. "Ken?" he cried.

"Yeah, Dad," Ken said.

"Why, you're a full grown man," Ed Talbot cried out in disbelief.

"I'm past my eighteenth birthday, yeah," Ken said.

"Well, I'll be darned, if you ain't the spitting image of me when I was your age! Come on in. It's messy in here, but that won't come as no surprise," Dad said with a wry chuckle.

The front room contained a couple of sagging couches, the stuffing oozing from the pillows like cream cheese. Threadbare rugs covered part of the cement floor. Fishing gear was lying around everywhere. The house smelled like fish and the salty sea.

"You know, Kenny, the weather folks are saying a big old hurricane is heading this way. I'll make some money boarding up windows in the next few days. You know—nailing up plywood over the glass before the owners hightail it to higher ground," Dad explained.

Ken glanced through one of the dirty windows. "Sun's sure shining now, Dad.

Chapter • 2

Doesn't look much like a hurricane out there to me," he said.

Dad laughed. He was missing a few more teeth than when Ken last saw him. "The weather people got these satellites, you know. They can see a hurricane coming from a long way off. 'Course, she could turn and miss us altogether."

"What do you do when a hurricane comes?" Ken asked.

"Just board up the windows and sit tight. I don't leave. When my number is up, I figure the good Lord is gonna find me wherever I am," Dad laughed.

The ocean wasn't too far away. If a hurricane did raise big waves, it wouldn't be much of a stretch to imagine this house washing away. But Ken wasn't much of a worrier, either. Mom and his stepdad worried about *everything*—burglars, the stock market, getting old, you name it. Ken didn't see the sense of it.

"So, tell me what you've been doing, Kenny," Dad said, popping open two soda cans and handing one to Ken.

"I tried college but I didn't like it," Ken said.

"Flunked, huh?" Dad asked with a knowing look.

"Yeah," Ken said. He didn't mind admitting his failures to Dad. Dad knew all about losing. Wasn't Mom always saying that? *"You're a loser, a failure, you're not worth warm spit,"* Mom had screamed at Dad during their final argument. "You know, Dad, sitting in the classroom's just not for me," he said. "I've had some jobs I've liked. I worked at the zoo. That was cool. Maybe I'll get a job dealing with animals. I love animals. I've read a lot of books on that kind of job. Maybe I could do something for endangered animals—like the big sea turtles on the Cayman Islands."

"So, how long are you planning on

Chapter • 2

staying here, Kenny?" Dad asked.

Ken shrugged. "Long as you can stand me, I guess. My half-brothers, Alex and Lew, sure won't miss me. They were already fighting over my room before I left," he said.

Dad nodded and said, "You're welcome here."

"I don't know where I'll end up," Ken said, "but I'm never going home to Mom and my stepdad." He knew that when he caught that bus he was leaving for good. He wouldn't *ever* be going back there again.

There were things about George Garvin that Ken would not even tell his father. Ken thought that would be disloyal to Mom. But the fact was, Garvin was downright *mean*. When he didn't like you, that was it—you could do no right. From the first day they met, there had been bad blood between them. Ken resented the man who'd come to take Dad's place, so he was a rude little boy. Garvin never made allowances for the boy's pain over losing his father. They were enemies from day one and it remained that way.

Dad turned on the radio for the latest weather news. The reporter said the hurricane was forming in the Caribbean. "It's moving north about twelve miles per hour," the weather forecaster said. "More news at ten."

"Well," Dad said, "it could still miss us. But if it *does* get here, it could be a big, bad blowhard."

"You ever been in a hurricane before, Dad?" Ken asked.

"Yeah, about five years ago. It blew half my house away. A beam came down and nearly split my skull." Dad took off his baseball cap, revealing an ugly scar at his hairline. "Thought I was a goner, for sure. But the good Lord had other ideas, I guess. My neighbor, Cal,

Chapter • 2

he found me the next day and patched me up."

"Man," Ken said, "why didn't you tell me about that?"

He shuddered at the thought that he could have lost his father. And he wouldn't have known until it was over.

"I didn't want to saddle you with it, Kenny," Dad said in a suddenly heavy voice. He looked very sad. "I know you had enough on your plate, boy. Your life ain't been no bed of roses."

"Oh, it's been fine," Ken lied.

"You know, Kenny, I don't have many regrets in life—but how things worked out for you is a *big* regret. I know I never was there for you, and that was bad. That was evil. . . ." Dad looked away.

Chapter 3

"It wasn't your fault. Mom never wanted you there, Dad," Ken said. When they had lived in Tampa, Mom always invented excuses why Ken couldn't go out with his father. Then Mom had moved the family up north to Detroit. She hoped Ed Talbot wouldn't be able to leave his fishing business to travel that far. Her plan had worked. Little by little, Dad had faded from the picture.

"I shoulda tried harder to see you, Kenny. It was wrong to just give up like I did. I just *shouldn't* have," Dad said, shaking his head sadly.

Ken walked around Breeze End in the afternoon. Dad had promised to take him along on his next fishing charter

Chapter • 3

trip. That way Ken could earn a little money of his own. But Ken was hoping he'd find another job in town. He didn't want to be a burden on his father. He had felt like a burden in his own house for too long.

Ken peered into the bait and tackle shop. "You don't need any help, do you? I'm looking for work."

A chubby woman pointed down the road to a small cafe. "They might be able to use a counter guy when the tourists start coming around. 'Course right now everybody's worried about the big storm that's comin'. Nobody's thinkin' of much else."

Ken went into the cafe. A swarthy man said, "See me after the storm—*if* this place is still standing! When it starts to blow around here, we don't stick around. Everyone with any sense heads out for higher ground."

Ken walked toward the ocean then.

The waves were pretty gentle now. There was no sign that in just a few days giant waves could be washing over this beach, driven by hundred-mile-per-hour winds. It didn't seem possible that the houses and businesses sitting there so peacefully could be broken up like matchsticks.

As Ken neared the water's edge, he saw a dark-haired girl in blue jeans and a red tank top. She was wading in the surf. Ken thought she looked pretty, at least from a distance.

"Hi," Ken called out to her when he was close enough to be heard above the soft rumble of the incoming tide.

The girl turned. "Hi," she said in a listless voice.

She *was* pretty. Her big, brown eyes seemed kind of sad, though. "I'm Amy."

"Heard about the big hurricane that's supposed to be coming?" Ken asked. "Uh . . . I'm Ken Talbot. I just got to

Chapter • 3

town. I'm staying with my dad."

The girl stared at Ken for a long moment. Then she said, "I hope the hurricane gets here fast. I hope it's a big one, too. They say that when a big hurricane is about to strike, the sky turns a terrible orchid color. I don't know for sure if that's so, but I can't wait to watch it all happen—to see the wind smashing everything down."

Ken wasn't sure he had heard her right. Her attitude was hard to figure. "You *like* the excitement, huh?"

"Not especially. I just hope I blow away," Amy said.

"Huh?" Ken asked, shocked. He drew a little closer. "Are you joking or what?"

"No, I'm not joking. I *should* be dead right now. It was a mistake that I lived and she didn't," Amy said. For some reason, the girl was trembling in the sunshine as if it were bitter cold!

21

The Terrible Orchid Sky

Worried, Ken saw that the girl seemed desperate to talk about what was bothering her.

"*Who* didn't live?" he asked softly.

"My best friend, Josie. We were best friends forever. She was better than any sister. I talked her into taking her mom's car so we could go joyriding one night. You could talk Josie into anything—*I* could, anyway. Josie was a really gentle and sweet girl. She would do anything you asked. She was an angel—and that makes me a devil," Amy said.

"Oh, I'm sure you're not a devil," Ken laughed nervously.

"Yeah, I am. I insisted on driving the car because I wanted to show off. I was driving real fast when the wheels slipped off the road and dumped us into the soft sand. That's why we turned over. Josie didn't have her seat belt on. I hadn't even had the decency to remind her to buckle up. She fell out of the car

Chapter • 3

and got crushed. I wasn't even hurt. How fair is that?" Amy asked, her voice harsh and near breaking.

"But you didn't *mean* for it to happen," Ken said, knowing how lame those words sounded. He sure wouldn't have wanted to be in Amy's shoes.

"But I'm *always* doing bad things. I'm an evil person, and that was the last straw," Amy insisted.

"You shouldn't be so hard on yourself, Amy," Ken said. "We all make mistakes—sometimes terrible mistakes."

Amy looked at him. "Your name is Ken, right? Well look, Ken, I skipped school all the time and I stole stuff from stores and cussed my parents out. Then two months ago I killed Josie. I should have gone to jail, but they said it was an accident so I just lost my license. Everybody was so nice to me. But I didn't deserve it.

"I *know* what I deserve," Amy said

bitterly. "I should blow away in that hurricane and sink to the bottom of the ocean and be eaten by sharks." Then she turned away.

Chapter 4

"I bet if Josie were standing here right now, *she'd* forgive you," Ken said. "And if she was such a good friend as you say, you know that she'd want you to forgive yourself."

"You're right," Amy said sadly. "She probably *would* forgive the devil." Then, turning sharply, she ran down the beach toward a cluster of apartment buildings. Ken watched her vanish into one of the downstairs apartments, the one with a pot of pink geraniums out front.

Maybe she was making it all up, Ken thought. Maybe the whole tale was a lie. A lot of young kids say crazy things just to get attention. Bewildered, Ken shook his head and walked slowly back up the road to his father's house.

Dad was shelling a bucket of shrimp in the front yard. Although Ken had never shelled shrimp before, he quickly got the hang of it.

"Easy now," Dad said. "Don't yank too hard or you won't have the whole shrimp anymore. Then, when I take the broken shrimp down to the packer, they don't want to pay me. Look, Kenny—a shrimp's shell is like paper. Be real gentle lifting it off." Dad watched Ken practice for a few seconds and then said, "*That's* the way, son. You're a natural born sheller!"

"Anything new on the hurricane?" Ken asked.

"She's still coming this way. I think we're gonna take a real big hit. Could be another few days, though," Dad said.

"Dad, I met this girl named Amy on the beach. She was telling me quite a tale—" Ken started to say.

Chapter • 4

Dad cut him off sharply. "Yeah, I know all about her. Amy Frost. Lives with her mother over in the Breeze End Villas. I remember when she was a little girl, climbing on the boats, making trouble, always making trouble. A regular little hellcat. She was in a real bad car accident a couple of months ago. Got little Josie McNair killed. Sweet little Josie—she shouldn't have had to die because of that brat," Dad's voice trembled with anger and bitterness.

Ken was startled by Dad's harsh words. "She seems really sorry, Dad," he said. "She even said she hopes the hurricane blows her away."

Dad nodded. "She's been nothing but bad news around here. She's raised a lot of hell, and I expect she's got some coming to her now." Again, Ken was surprised by the fury in Dad's voice. He usually wasn't that kind of man at all. He was almost always easygoing. That was one of the qualities that Ken most admired about his father. The man could always go with the flow. Nothing seemed to put him in a bad mood.

"It was an *accident*, though, Dad," Ken said defensively.

Dad stopped peeling the shrimp. He gave Ken a hard look. "When you mess around with drugs and booze and steal everything that ain't nailed down and give your family all that grief, a car crash ain't no *accident*. *Think* about it, Kenny. It's something that's bound to happen. She talked a poor innocent girl into sharing her wild, risky escapade, and that girl ended up dead. So tell me, son. Does that sound like an accident— or is it the natural end of a long string of evil pranks?" Dad demanded.

"But Dad, she really does seem to feel terrible about it," Ken insisted. By now, he was getting so good at peeling shrimp that his bucket was filling up

Chapter • 4

quite a bit faster than his father's.

"Josie McNair was my sister's child," Dad said sadly. "She was my niece, and I loved her like a daughter."

Ken gasped. He had never really known his father's family. Even when Ken's parents were married, Mom's family was the only one coming around. Ken vaguely knew his dad had an older sister, but he had never met her.

"Your Aunt Lee," Dad said, seeing the puzzlement on Ken's face. "You wouldn't remember her. She held you once when you were a baby. Josie was the sunshine of her parents' lives. Of *my* life, too. And she was the only child they ever had. . . ."

"Do Josie's parents still live in Breeze End?" Ken asked.

"No, they pulled up stakes right after the accident. Moved to Clearwater. I miss 'em something fierce. Lots of times the three of them used to come over and go fishing with me. Sometimes we'd dig a mess of clams and bake 'em. Those people were the only family I had in the last ten years," Dad said with real grief in his voice.

"That's awful, Dad," Ken said. "I'm really sorry."

The sun was beginning to go down now, turning the billowing clouds pink and gold. Ken watched the gulls flying against the darkening sky.

"If the storm comes," Dad said, "it'll start with clouds, then steady rain and thunderstorms. Then the storm will get bigger and bigger. Those waves could get forty feet high. When we see the waves getting real high, we know for certain the hurricane is bearing down."

Dad turned around and looked right at his son. "You know, Kenny, it's one thing to risk this worthless old hide of mine—but when we hear for sure that the hurricane is about to hit, *you* better

Chapter • 4

git outta here quick."

"No," Ken said, "I want to stay."

"You never been in one of these storms, Kenny. You don't know what you're in for," Dad said seriously.

Ken smiled. "I just got here, Dad. I'm not leaving for any reason, okay? It took some guts for me to leave the only home I ever knew. You can bet I got what it takes to stare down a big wind."

Chapter 5

Ken couldn't get Amy off his mind. He had spent most of his life being down on himself. Of course, he never had to deal with anything like causing the death of a friend—but he knew he was a big disappointment to his mom. There were times when he might have welcomed a big wind to blow him off the planet, too. Ken felt sorry for somebody as bummed out as Amy was.

So Ken decided to find the girl and try to cheer her up. That night, he walked down to the Breeze End Villas. If Amy was hanging around outside, Ken thought, he might strike up a conversation with her. Sometimes just talking about it seemed to make a

Chapter • 5

problem a little more bearable.

Ken didn't see the girl outside, so he rapped on the door of the apartment he thought he had seen her enter.

A thin, pretty woman opened the door. "Yeah?" She looked like she might be Amy's mother. She had the same big, sad eyes.

"Is Amy home?" Ken asked.

The woman looked Ken up and down in a hostile way. Ken wore an old t-shirt with the frantic faces of a rap band emblazened on the front. His jeans were ratty, with his knee peeking through a big hole. "Yeah," the woman said, "you look like the kinda trash she likes to hang out with. Josie McNair was the only decent friend she ever had—and look what happened to her."

"Where is Amy?" Ken asked.

"How should I know? She comes and goes as she likes. I'm only her mother. She never tells me what she's doing or where she's going. Are you one of her boyfriends? Don't think I've ever seen you before," the woman said.

"No, ma'am. I just moved down here from Detroit. I don't even know your daughter. I just met her on the beach today. She seemed to be awful depressed. I guess I felt sort of worried about her," Ken said.

"Maybe she's taken off again," Amy's mother said. "She does that sometimes. I work hard waitressing, and I've done my best with her—but I've given up. Her father has run off, too. I don't know where either of them are, and I don't much care. Worrying over Amy is getting old." Then the door closed abruptly in Ken's face.

As Ken headed home, he noticed that the waves were higher and the wind was picking up. He kept his eyes peeled for Amy. In spite of what everybody said, Ken felt sorry for her. *The poor girl*

Chapter • 5

was a loser. Ken could identify with that. He had always been a loser, too.

When Ken got home without seeing anything of Amy, his father said, "You better call your mother. She's been looking for you. They're talking about the hurricane on the national news and she's worried."

Ken dialed his home in Detroit. "Mom?" he said. "What's up?"

"Ken, we've been listening to the weather news on TV. There's a terrible hurricane coming toward the east coast of Florida. You've got to get out of there right now!" Mom cried.

"It's okay, Mom," Ken reassured her. "Dad and I are boarding up the windows, and we'll be just fine. Don't worry. Dad's real cool about it."

"But Ed Talbot is a *fool!*" Mom snapped. "He's always been a fool about everything. I want you to get out of there, and come home *now*! Just because your father was a little harsh with you was no reason for you to run out of here like that."

"George is *not* my father," Ken corrected her. "I'm with my father now, and I'm just fine, okay?"

"You're doing this to punish me, aren't you?" Mom asked sadly.

"No, Mom. I just want to try something new, you know? I need some time. Listen, if the storm gets too bad I'll go to the evacuation center, okay?" Ken said.

"Promise me you won't wait until it's too late," Mom said.

"I won't," Ken promised. "Talk to you later, Mom." When he hung up, he caught his dad staring at him.

"Kenny, I wouldn't think any less of you if you took off right now. You know that, don't you?" Dad said.

"Sure, Dad," Ken said. "I've seen television coverage of hurricanes, the

Chapter • 5

palm trees flattened, everything blowing around. I guess it's scary—but not as scary as it was going to Marshall High, I'll tell you that."

Dad's eyebrows went up. "What're you talking about, Kenny? Marshall wasn't a *bad* school."

"You ever notice I'm not as tall as most guys, Dad? And I'm a tad skinny, right? You don't want to know what it was like being the shortest, skinniest kid in most every class. You don't wanna know how many times I was slammed against lockers or got dirty gym socks stuffed in my face. I was laughed at and half choked and messed up every day," Ken said.

"*Kenny!*" Dad said shakily.

"Hurricanes? Man, they don't bother me. Six foot two football players, now *there's* terror—especially when they got your shirtfront bunched up in their hammy fists!" Ken said.

Chapter 6

"Did you ever tell your mom about what was happening at school?" Dad asked.

Ken shook his head. "That would have given ol' George something else to rag me about. He already thought I was stupid and lazy. Only a coward can't fight his own battles. You know what old George looks like—bull neck, big thick arms. He thinks he's so tough. *Nobody* messes with George Garvin and gets away with it," Ken said.

"I shoulda been there," Dad said. "I woulda taught you how to fight, to take care of yourself. When I was young, I was on the scrawny side myself."

Suddenly Ken heard something

Chapter • 6

strange. Earlier, the waves washing up on the beach had made a gentle pleasing sound. Now the sound was almost a roar, like growling thunder. "What's that noise?" Ken asked.

"Storm whipping up the ocean," Dad said, opening the front door and looking outside. Ken could see the foam whipping off the waves. "Looks like she's coming, boy. The weather folks knew what they were talking about."

They turned on the radio. The forecaster said the eastern islands were in line for a direct hit. Her voice was tense. The eastern islands trailed down from Miami toward Key West like a string of uneven beads. Breeze End lay in the bull's eye of the oncoming storm.

"I did some carpentry work at the zoo, Dad," Ken said. "I'm pretty handy with a hammer and nails. Tomorrow I can help you board up windows." Ken's heart was beating a little faster now that he could actually see the early signs of the storm coming. The worst weather he'd ever seen in Tampa was a heavy thunderstorm. In Detroit he had seen some big snowstorms. But this would be a *hurricane*—something really dangerous.

But Ken wasn't really afraid. Not now. Not yet.

Early the next morning there were some clouds, but the sun was shining. It looked like a nice, ordinary day.

"Hurricanes, they'll fool you," Dad said. "You look at the sky and think everything is just fine. But she's out there, blowing and spouting, just like a confounded woman carrying a big bag of dirty tricks."

Ken wondered just then if Dad thought Mom had a bag of dirty tricks. He couldn't imagine two such different people getting married at all. Mom always valued the material things of life. She wanted the nicest home, the best

Chapter • 6

furniture, the newest car. Dad was content with just getting by. Maybe when Mom fell in love with Dad, she didn't know how it would be. Maybe she used her bag of dirty tricks to convince Dad to marry her.

Then later, Ken thought, she had been mighty sorry. . . .

As Ken and his father went from place to place covering big plate glass windows with sheets of plywood, the wind kept picking up. The merchants were impatient to see their stores protected so they could get out of town.

"Dad," Ken said, "I asked Mom a couple of years ago how come she married you. She never would say. She'd just tell me she had been a fool. You got a better answer, Dad?"

Dad plucked a nail from his belt and hammered away. Then he laughed, "I was just eighteen. She was seventeen. That's your answer right there, boy.

The Terrible Orchid Sky

You're dumb as a lobster when you're seventeen or eighteen—least about the kind of person you want to marry. I had me a little boat then and we'd go sailing. Your mom thought that was peachy. We fell in love, I guess. But love is the flimsiest reason of all for two young people to marry, Kenny."

When the man who owned the hardware store inspected the protected window, he nodded approvingly. "Good job, Talbot. I hope the place will be okay when we get back. We're leaving right away, just as soon as I pay you. I've got the car all packed. Sure don't want to wait until the highway gets crowded. We could easily get trapped in a line of stalled cars!"

Dad divided the money with Ken, and they moved on to the next place. They spent the whole morning boarding up stores and houses.

"We got to thank this old hurricane

Chapter • 6

for putting plenty of change in our pockets, Kenny," Dad said with a grin. "One man's meat is another man's poison. 'Course she may end up tossing us both into Davy Jones' locker—and we'll have no use for money there!"

Ken laughed. His father wasn't taking the hurricane seriously, and that cheered Ken. It seemed natural to take on the same attitude. For a long time he had been nothing but a victim of his stepdad's contempt and his classmates' abuse. Now, at long last, Ken felt like a *man*, laughing in the teeth of a storm.

As the day drew on, the darkening sky began to change. It was taking on that strange color Amy had described—a bruised violet shade.

"There she is," Dad said. "Look at it, son. Look at the terrible orchid sky."

Chapter 7

As Ken and his father covered the cafe windows with plywood, Amy's mother came out with a big man who locked the door behind them. She was a waitress at the cafe, but now there was no one there to serve. All that morning, she'd sold takeout sandwiches to the fleeing families. But nobody else would be coming by now—not until after the storm was over.

"Has either of you guys seen my daughter?" the woman asked, not recognizing Ken. "I'm leaving town in an hour, and I've got to find her. She took off yesterday, and I don't know where she is." Amy's mother seemed concerned now.

Chapter • 7

"Oh, don't sweat it, Brownie," the middle-aged owner of the cafe said. He was Amy's mother's boss and her new boyfriend as well. "That little gal can take care of herself. She probably hitched a ride with some trucker. She's likely to be halfway to Miami by now, snug as a bug in a rug."

"I don't know," Amy's mother said nervously. "I'd hate to think she was hiding out in the scrub palmettoes. If she is, what's she gonna do when the storm comes?"

The man laughed. "Not Amy. She's a sharp one. That girl's sixteen going on forty." The man put a protective arm around Amy's mother. "Let's just get our things, Brownie, and then we'll head out, too. Believe me, your Amy's long gone down the road."

A light rain began to fall as the sun went down. The heavy stream of traffic leaving Breeze End had now thinned

The Terrible Orchid Sky

down to a trickle. Most of the residents and all of the tourists staying in the only motel were already gone.

"Only the fools are still here," said Cal, Dad's crony, as darkness covered the land. He lived in a house about a hundred yards behind Dad's house. His place was even more broken down than Ed Talbot's was.

The sheriff's car made another run through town. Its loudspeakers blared out in grim tones, "Everybody should evacuate Breeze End and move on to protected inland areas. The latest weather advisory warns that the hurricane will come ashore around three tomorrow morning."

Cal chuckled. "Sheriff Moe ain't fool enough to think he can drive old land crabs like us away, Ed," he said.

"Yeah, look," Dad laughed, "now *he's* hightailing it out of here, too."

Cal headed back to his own boarded-

Chapter • 7

up shack. Ken and his father turned toward home then, just as the rain began to come down with a harder beat.

"Good thing we're stocked up with plenty of canned goods," Dad said once they went inside. "Looks like we'll be eating lots of peanut butter sandwiches and canned ham for a while."

"The electricity will probably go out, huh, Dad?" Ken asked a bit nervously.

"Yeah, falling tree limbs are sure to pull the wires down. But we got flashlights and lots of batteries for just such special occasions," Dad chuckled.

The rain was growing heavier by the minute. It sounded like dozens of little hammers pounding on the roof. Ken had never heard such driving rain.

Then, in the midst of the pounding rain, Ken and his father heard another sound—a plaintive cry.

Ken pictured some poor dog or cat caught out there in the wild weather.

"What's that sound, Dad?" he asked.

"Maybe a cat. Lot of stray cats hang around here. Some poor critter probably got frightened out of her wits," Dad said, yanking open the door. The wind was so strong it almost ripped the door from Dad's hold.

"*You!*" Dad growled. "What do you want? How dare you come here?"

Ken couldn't immediately see who was at the door. Then he looked around Dad's shoulder and saw the girl—Amy. She was drenched to the skin, her hair plastered to her scalp. With her lower lip trembling from cold and fear, she whimpered, "I-I'm so s-scared!"

Ken stared from the girl to his father. He knew how bitter his father felt about this girl. After all, her recklessness had cost him his beloved niece. But Ken felt sure he wouldn't turn her away. Not *now*. Not in this storm.

"Amy Frost, you're bad to the bone,"

Chapter • 7

Dad snarled at the wet, trembling girl.

Ken opened his mouth to plead the girl's cause, but he stopped himself. He had to trust his father enough to do the right thing without prodding. Then, suddenly, Dad swung the door wide and said, "Okay, get in here, but don't make no trouble! Just be quiet and you can wait out the storm. After that, you *git*—hear me?"

Amy nodded, scurrying over to the far corner of the room where she sat on the floor, shivering. Looking over at her, Ken remembered her wish. She had hoped that the hurricane would sweep her off into the ocean and end all her troubles. Now he saw that she had a will to live after all. Down deep inside, she was just a scared little girl.

Ken found an old blanket in a closet and brought it to her. "Here. Put this around you. I think you've got a nervous chill, Amy. This should help."

The Terrible Orchid Sky

"Thanks," she said, stealing an anxious glance across the room at Ed Talbot. He appeared to be taking some quick shut-eye.

"You been hiding out somewhere, Amy?" Ken asked. "Your mom was looking all over for you."

"I planned to *stay* hidden, too. But I messed it all up, as usual," Amy groaned. "Look at me—I couldn't even *die* right! I had to chicken out and come looking for help!"

Chapter 8

"Come on, Amy, don't be like that," Ken said.

"My mom's got a new boyfriend," Amy said. "I can't stand him. He's such a sleaze. I made up my mind to stay out there in the palmetto grove. Then, when the weather got bad, I thought about you—about how nice you were to me even when you knew what I'd done. So I figured maybe you'd let me in for a little while."

"It'll be okay now, Amy. I'm glad you did," Ken said.

Huddling in the threadbare blanket, Amy said nothing.

"You ever been in a hurricane before?" Ken asked her.

"Once. It smashed our garage, but nobody got hurt. That was when Mom and Dad were still together. I was about ten or eleven. When I think back about those days, I guess I must have been the happiest kid alive—even though I didn't know it then," Amy said, her eyes filling with sadness. "Ken, do you ever think back to a time you were so happy that it makes you just *ache* to remember it?"

"I don't think so," Ken admitted.

"Not *ever*?" Amy asked. "What about before your parents split up?"

"I was only five years old. I don't remember all that much, except that they were fighting a lot. That's all I can remember—the awful fights," Ken said.

"I was much older than that when my folks split up," Amy said. "It really hurt me, because I was so crazy about my dad. He was real good to me. But he had fallen for another woman, and before long he left Mom. He still sends

Chapter • 8

me birthday cards, but I don't answer them. One time he wrote that he and his new wife had a baby girl. I tore up that letter into a million pieces and threw it in the ocean for the fish to eat!"

"Fish don't eat paper," Ken said, trying to comfort her by lightening up the conversation.

"Well, maybe the octopuses ate it," Amy said stubbornly.

"Octopuses sit in their lairs in crevices or rocks and wait for crabs to come by so they can eat them," Ken said. "Did you know that octopuses can change color real fast? They can change from green to dark purple, and then to white as a ghost in just a few seconds."

Amy looked at Ken, wide-eyed. "How do you know all that? You must be really smart," she said. It was the first time that Ken could remember that anybody ever called him *smart*. "No," he said, "I've actually been told I'm pretty dumb. It's just that I'm really interested in animals, and I read a lot of books about them."

After a while, Amy and Ken dozed off on the floor. Then, just before dawn, the hurricane hit Breeze End. Just as the weather people had predicted, it struck with a terrible, shattering force. In a few seconds, the neighbor's porch came crashing into the wall right next to the corner spot where Ed Talbot had been sleeping! Both Amy and Ken leaped to their feet in sheer terror. Then the lights went out, and everything around them was in total darkness.

Now rain poured in the gaping hole that had been torn in the roof and outside wall. Ken groped for his flashlight. *"Dad!"* he shouted. "You okay? *Dad!"* Ken swept the far corner of the room with his flashlight beam. The place where Ed Talbot had been sleeping on the floor was now piled high with

Chapter • 8

debris. "*Dad!*" Ken screamed in terror.

Amy found another flashlight and scrambled after Ken, shining the beam of the light before her. But their path was totally blocked by fallen chunks of ragged wood. They could see that the wind had driven the porch into the house, bringing down a wall and part of the roof.

"Dad's under there," Ken sobbed. "Amy, the house came down on him! I can't even see him!" Ken knelt on the floor, while Amy held the flashlight. He clawed at the wood, trying to clear a path to his father.

The horror of the situation made it hard for Ken to breathe. He had waited six years to see his dad again. He'd been here just a few days, and now maybe Dad was dead . . . crushed by the fallen debris!

"We've got to get help!" Amy cried.

Ken jumped up and ran to the

phone. But it was purely a reflex action. He might have known it would be dead. Then he ran to the window and looked outside. Like so many writhing snakes, the phone and electric wires lay in a tangled mess at the bottom of the shattered power poles.

Now Ken realized that it could be a very long time before rescue workers got to Breeze End. Any help they'd get was going to have to come from themselves.

"Amy, hold the flashlight over toward the corner where Dad's buried. I've *got* to get that stuff off him. Maybe he's still alive," Ken gasped. Now he was breathing hard from the exertion of trying to drag the heavy chunks of wood away from the corner. Ken cut his hands on nails sticking from the jagged wood. He ignored the blood streaming down his wrists and onto his shirt. He just kept yanking at the debris, trying to uncover his father. "Dad! Can you hear

Chapter • 8

me? I'm gonna get you out, Dad. Hang on! I'm gonna get you out, okay?"

Then, from deep beneath the pile of debris, a voice rang out sharply. "Get back!" Dad commanded. "Don't come any closer, Kenny. I got a big old roof beam on my leg and I'm trapped. There's a lot of heavy wood just dangling over me. You gotta get *out*, boy! The whole house is ready to go. If it falls down on you, you'll be a goner just like me. *Run*, Kenny!"

Chapter 9

Ken felt sick with fear. "Dad, are you hurt bad?" he called out.

"Feels like I'm half crushed, Kenny. There's no help for me, but you can save your own life, and you got to do it now. Do you hear me, boy? There's a little cement block shed behind Cal's house. Run there and hide inside. She should stand up against the hurricane. I'm sure you'll be okay there," Dad said in a shaky voice.

"No way, Dad. I'm not leaving you!" Ken cried.

"I'm telling you, Kenny, you'll *die* here—just like me. I don't want my son to die in this hurricane! You got to get out before the whole roof comes down

Chapter • 9

on your head!" Dad pleaded. "It's my fault you're still here. I shoulda made you leave. It's all my fault!"

Ken turned to Amy. "You heard what he said. Run to the shed and take shelter there while you can," he said.

Amy's eyes were huge. She held the flashlight in a trembling hand. "I killed the only person he ever cared about, and now *I* should abandon him, too? No way, Ken. I finally have a chance to make up a little for what I did. I *gotta* stay and help!"

Ken didn't have time to argue. He knew the house could collapse at any minute. He *had* to try to get Dad out before that happened.

"Okay, Amy, hold the flashlight steady," Ken said. He continued pulling the boards away from his father. As he yanked off a piece of roofing paper, Ken yelled, "*I see him,* Amy! His right leg is pinned and it's bleeding!"

59

The Terrible Orchid Sky

Dad was deathly pale. In a whispery, weakened voice he pleaded with Ken to save himself. "You can't get me out, boy. Save *yourself*! You're just a kid! You got your whole life ahead of you. You're my son. I love you, Kenny. I won't have you dying to save this worthless old hide of mine. I'm not worth it, Kenny. I've been a lousy dad, a lousy man!"

"Shut up, Dad . . . save your strength," Ken said. He looked around. Somehow he needed to pry the beam off Dad's leg and drag him out of here.

Amy pushed her way beside him, dragging a solid wooden plank behind her. "What do you think, Ken? Would this work as a lever? Could you squeeze it under the beam and lift it just a little? Then I could try to pull him free. I'm strong, and he's not a big man. Maybe it'd work," she said hopefully.

Ken forced the plank under the beam that pinned his father to the floor. With

Chapter • 9

all his strength he tried to raise it, but it barely moved. "I gotta get it up," he gasped. After all these years he had finally found his dad. He couldn't bear to lose him now. He just *couldn't*.

Amy's face was wet and dirty. Blood trickled from her cheek where a splinter had torn the skin. But now she grabbed Dad's body under his arms. She was just a little thing, however. How could she pull a 140-pound man out from under the heavy beam?

Ken pressed down on the plank, trying desperately to raise the beam higher. But it seemed hopeless. Even if he lifted it up for a second or two, how could Amy pull Dad free? "Amy, you can't do it," Ken groaned.

"I can!" Amy shouted. "I tell you I *can!*" Her voice was unnatural, like a growl from an animal's throat. Amy felt ferocious in her determination. She had been through so much—the drugs, the liquor, the running away. She had been so angry, so depressed. When she saw the body of her dead friend, she had sunk lower than she ever thought possible. But now she glimpsed a chance to redeem herself. She had been sure she'd never get another chance—but now, here it was. *Nobody* was going to take it from her!

Ken used every ounce of strength he had to pry up the beam. Amy pulled with all her might. Once the pressure was off, Ed Talbot screamed in pain as the blood ran into his injured leg. Then Amy pulled him free.

Working together, Ken and Amy dragged the man across the floor. As they inched along, the relentlessly howling wind continued to batter the nearly demolished house. Ken knew they had to get out immediately. As they reached the door, they saw that dawn was lightening the sky. They were in the

Chapter • 9

eye of the storm now. Inside the eye, the skies cleared a little and the winds died down. Then, when the next winds hit, they would be coming from the opposite direction. Once again ferocious rains would attack the land. But right now there was a brief period of calm.

Ken looked out the window at the tiny concrete shed behind Cal's house. It wasn't big enough for all three of them. But strangely, Dad's pickup truck stood nearly undamaged near the house. It was covered by palm fronds, and its hood was dented, but maybe it still ran!

"Come on, Amy," Ken cried. "Help me get Dad in the camper shell." Once this was done, Ken got behind the wheel, praying the truck would start. The engine turned over and they drove off toward town. Since flying debris had ripped three of the four tires, Ken drove on the rims. He was heading for the hardware store. It was a cement block building that had a good chance of still being there.

At the hardware store, Ken broke down the back door. Soon he and Amy had carried Dad inside.

"He needs a doctor bad," Amy said. "Look how his leg is bleeding."

"We gotta *do* something, Amy," Ken said, frantically. "Do you know anything about first aid?"

"I took this dumb little course in high school," Amy said. "I don't know if I remember anything, though."

Amy and Ken rushed around the store, finding fabric and masking tape. Soon they had elevated Dad's leg and made a snug bandage around his bleeding calf. Although the bleeding didn't stop, the flow was reduced to oozing instead of flowing.

"He seems awful cold," Ken said nervously, terrified that after all this, they could end up losing Dad anyway.

Chapter • 9

"It could be shock," Amy said. "Get some blankets over in the camping section, Ken. We gotta cover him up." Bits and pieces of her first aid class were slowly returning to her.

Ken glanced over at his dad. He looked awfully pale and still. "No, Dad," Ken whispered as he ran to get the blankets. "Not now. *Don't die now . . . please don't!*"

Chapter 10

After they covered Dad with blankets, Amy and Ken huddled together in the dark hardware store. Silently they listened to the storm as it crashed around outside like a deadly beast on a rampage.

"Amy, I don't know what I woulda done without you," Ken said. "I couldn't have saved my dad. . . ."

"No, you saved *me*," Amy insisted. "If you and your dad hadn't let me in last night, I would've been swept into the ocean."

"You were terrific, Amy," Ken said.

Amy drew up her knees and moved closer to him. "You know what, Ken? For the first time since Josie died, I don't

Chapter • 10

feel like I should absolutely, positively die, too. I know your dad will be okay, Ken. Just think—if you hadn't been here, he *woulda* died. He woulda been in the house alone with nobody to help him, and he woulda died for sure. And if we hadn't met that day and you hadn't been nice to me, *I* wouldn't have been here to help you. Maybe there *is* a plan, huh, Ken? Maybe we all got a purpose—do you think?"

It was nearly midday now, and the relentless winds had slowed to short gusts. The drenching rain was now just a steady, soft drizzle. Ken heard the rumbling of a four-wheel drive and he rushed outside to see the sheriff.

"You darn fools!" the sheriff yelled crossly. "You stayed in Breeze End through it all!"

"We need a doctor," Ken shouted to the sheriff. "My dad is hurt."

Within an hour the winds had died

down enough to permit a helicopter to land. It set down in the grocery store parking lot across from the hardware store. Ken, Amy, and Dad went off to the hospital, ending up in the emergency room. In a few minutes, Dad was pronounced in good shape, considering everything. His leg was not even broken. It was just severely lacerated—and, of course, he had lost a lot of blood.

The doctor said that Ed Talbot was a lucky fool, but he'd be back on his feet in a few days.

"Well, Kenny," Dad said when his son went in to see him, "you're a real hero. You saved this old man's life when I didn't deserve it. Your mom was probably right all along. I haven't got the sense I was born with. I *am* a stupid fool, and she was *right* to leave me! You just better hop on a bus and go home where you belong now, Kenny."

"I could've left, Dad," Ken said. "I

Chapter • 10

made up my own mind to stay for the hurricane, just like you did. I must be as big a fool as you are, Dad. That's why I'm staying in Breeze End. You and me, Dad—we're alike. For the first time in my life, I feel at home. I never knew where I belonged before . . . but now I know. It's with *you*, Dad."

When Ken and his father arrived back in Breeze End, the sun was shining on the terrible scene of destruction. Power saws were buzzing like millions of bees as felled trees and other debris were chopped up and hauled away.

It turned out that Cal's house had partially collapsed, too. But he had taken refuge in his concrete shed and had survived unhurt. Nobody at all had been killed in Breeze End because most everyone had gone to higher, safer ground. Of the few who remained, only Ken's father was injured badly enough to need hospital treatment.

Ken called his mother as soon as power was restored.

"Ken!" Mom said in a drained voice. "I'm sending you a plane ticket. I want you to come home at once. I've been worried sick listening to the news about that horrible hurricane."

"I'm fine, Mom," Ken assured her.

"Ken," Mom said in a serious voice, "your father and I *insist* that you come home right now—do you understand?"

"He's not my father, Mom. *You know that*. I promise you that I'm fine right here. I'm sorry you were worried, but I gotta go now. We have a lot of cleaning up to do," Ken said.

"Don't think you can dismiss me like that, Kenneth," Mom said.

"Love you, Mom," Ken said before he hung up.

There *was* a lot of work for Ken to do in the following weeks. He was making some nice money as a carpenter and clean-

Chapter • 10

up man, using Dad's pickup to haul debris out to the town dump. In fact, Ken made enough money to seriously think about signing up for community college in the fall. "If I could study animals, I think it might work, Dad. Who knows? Maybe I could find a career in conservation or work with animals in a zoo," he said.

"Good for you, Kenny," Dad said with a look of pride in his face.

"Dad, uh . . . Amy is doing better now, too. Her mom said she was really trying," Ken said.

"Well, I know she helped save *my* useless hide," Dad said slowly. "Tell her I'm grateful for that, will you?"

"You better tell her yourself, Dad. I know it would mean more coming from you," Ken said insistently.

"I'm not sure I've come that far yet, Kenny," Dad said, staring down at the sand at his feet.

Ken had been wanting to tell his

71

father something ever since he got there. But so far he had never found the right words. He was so glad to have found his dad and discovered that he was a good man. But now, finally, he realized how much he'd missed while he was growing up. His childhood was history. He could never get it back. And the sad truth was that *he had missed out*. In his loneliness and pain, he had reached out for a father time after time—but no father had been there.

"Dad, when I was a little kid, I kept hoping you'd find a way to be with me. You have no idea how much I hoped—every day and every night! I wanted a dad *so much*. But that's okay. I'm going to be okay now. I want you to know that I forgive you, Dad . . . and I love you. But I'll always miss the times you weren't there, you know?" Ken blinked back his tears.

Tears were running down Ed Talbot's

Chapter • 10

face, too. For a moment he swallowed hard and looked away. Then, bowing his head, he clasped his hands and nodded.

"Kenny," he said, "why don't you go ahead and send for Amy Frost. You tell her that we're having barbecued chicken tonight. Tell her that she and her mama are welcome to come for supper. And *I'll* tell her that I've forgiven her, too. I will do that, Kenny. . . ."

Then Ken did something he'd been longing to do all his life. He hugged the father he had never had, and his heart overflowed with love and hope.

COMPREHENSION QUESTIONS

COMPARING CHARACTERS

1. How was Ed Talbot different from George Garvin?

2. How was Amy Frost different from Josie McNair?

DRAWING CONCLUSIONS

1. When Ken arrived, why did Ed Talbot have trouble recognizing his own son?

2. Why did Ed Talbot think Amy's car wreck was "no accident"?

3. Why did Ken leave his home in Detroit?

CAUSE AND EFFECT

1. What effect do hurricane winds have on trees and buildings in the path?

2. What was the effect of Amy's midnight joyride?

3. What caused Ed Talbot to forgive Amy?

VOCABULARY

1. The story says there was "bad blood" between Ken Talbot and George Garvin. What is meant by the term *bad blood*?

2. Ed Talbot said that Ken was the "spitting image" of himself as a boy. What is meant by the term *spitting image*?

3. Ken promised his mom he would go to an "evacuation center" if the storm got bad. Why would people go to an *evacuation center*? What kind of place is it?

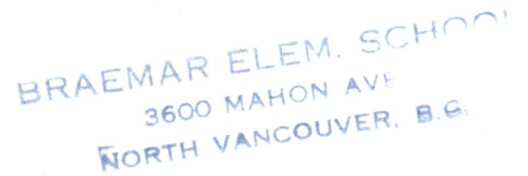